ISBN: 978-1-73696-084-4   Kindle Direct Edition

Testimonials

"Through wonderful drawings and simple to understand text, both adults and children can enjoy and learn about maintaining the health of one the most important systems of our bodies."

Dr Mayama Morehart, MD

"Thank you! I love when they met the King of Poo. It made me laugh so much. Thank you. Ha Ha Ha the King of Poop!! O Ha Ha Ha. The King of Poop! Oh Sorry, I got carried away. Thank you. It makes me imagen inside me! Thank you!"

Ana (age9)

"My students loved your book presentation. One of my students is keeping the book in her desk and thinks I don't know it. She reads it every chance she gets."

Idalia Stuart, first grade teacher.

"I really did enjoy reading the book- three times, like kids do. It's a wonderful read-aloud story and an excellent beginning for diet education."

Phil Filbrandt MD, Fellow American Board of Physical Medicine and Rehabilitation

"This is the book my daughter has been requesting for her bedtime story. It was delightful to watch light bulbs of understanding flash and see her interest in science develop as this story continued."

Ashley Harrison, DDS

I read it to my 8 year old granddaughter. She laughed and loved it. Then she re-read it by herself. I recommend it as a 'Must Have' for all children!"

Linda Nilsen R.N.

"A brilliant way to learn about two of the most overlooked factors in maintaining a healthy well nourished body: enzymes and the role probiotics play in digestive."

Dr Patrick Giammaries DC, HIS, LDHS, Digestion Relief Center, Chico CA

"What a wonderful, important book! Being aware of and caring for there bio-terrain is probably about the most important thing a person can do to assure good health."

Dr. Deborah Penner, DC Chico Creek Wellness Center

"Our two-year-old daughter loves this book-it's one of her favorites! We appreciate Janice Condon providing a story that's so fun and educational. I recently referenced it on my podcast."

-Rachel Maskell, Mumboss.com & James Maskell,
founder of the Functional Forum and Evolution of Medicine

About the Author

Jan Maximov Condon is a presently working Occupational Therapist with a keen interest in nutrition for wellness.

Her passion to share respect for gut microbes came from personal experience: the overuse of antibiotics in childhood and the problems it led to.

"Around middle age I suffered from skin rashes, weight loss, cloudy thinking, and a lack of energy. No doctor I visited addressed my gut as the source of my problems. Fortunately I found the local Weston A Price chapter. With nutrient dense and fermented food from the GAPS diet, my gut healed in 3 months. I will always be grateful to those kind and knowledgeable people."

Jan and her husband Frank enjoy an active lifestyle with jogging, swimming, yoga, and weight workouts.

They live in Chico, CA.

"Please visit my website:
 janmaxcon.com   for Song: Do the Acidophilus Hula!"

WRITTEN BY JANICE MAXIMOV CONDON

ILLUSTRATED BY STEVE FERCHAUD & CHRIS FICKEN

LULU MEETS THE KING OF POO

"Goodnight, Lulu." "Goodnight, Mom."

"Mom, I don't feel so good – kind of funny in the stomach."

"Was it that big piece of chocolate birthday cake?" asked Mom.

"I don't think so. Maybe it's the class science project. I don't have any ideas for it."

"Don't worry, dear, maybe you'll have a new idea when you wake up. I'll rub your tummy 'til you fall asleep."

So her mom rubbed her tummy, and Lulu fell into a deep sleep…

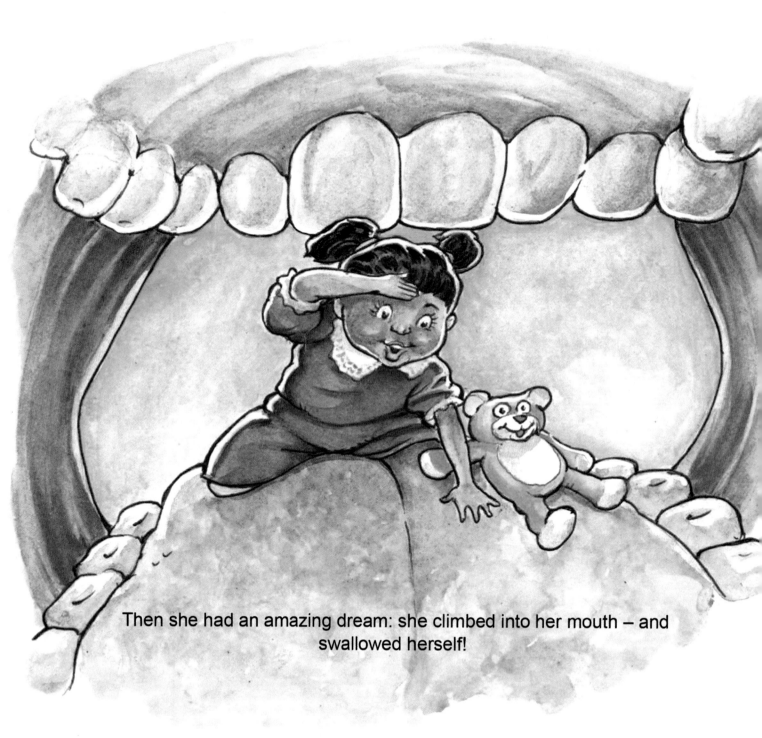

Then she had an amazing dream: she climbed into her mouth – and swallowed herself!

She tumbled down her throat,
and there she was in her own stomach.

"I'm Emily Enzyme, and this is my space.
How great that you've landed in just the right place.
Your science project is what you came for.
I'll give you an incredible, digestible tour!"

We enzymes start on your very first bite –
With saliva, your spittle! What a delight!
We break food down so your body can absorb it,
From soup to nuts, even Pineapple Shorbet!
We zap 'em! We snap 'em! We think we're pretty slick.
We change things, re-arrange things. Quicker than quick!

"Whoops! Here we go!
Out of the stomach, to Abby's world we'll go.
To the small intestine, down with the flow."

"We cling to the villi inside your gut wall.
We boost your immune system, and that's not all:
We prevent diarrhea; we make Vitamin B.
We are millions – so tiny, your eyes cannot see."

"What are villi?" asks Lulu.
"Little hills inside the gut walls." says Abby

"Gut acidophili further digest your food.
It digests way better when it's really well chewed.
Once chewed and digested, we give it a plus+
Then we hula it down to Benny Bifidus."

"Let's hula through the villi about 10 feet more,
To the Ileocecal (\ill-ee-o-\see-kul) valve – it's like a little door.
Once we get there, we'll squeeze on through –
Then you can meet Benny Bifidus, King of Poo!

The colon is the last stop before leaving your body.
That's why we also call him King of the Potty."

"EWWW!
The King of Poo!"

"Big Benny Bifidus, King of Poo! - at your service. How do you do?"

"Hi Benny, I'm Lulu - What an amazing trip so far!
Emily Enzyme, Abby Acidophilus, now you're the shining star!"

"Well I don't know if I'm a shining star.
But I do know what a great team we are!!"

"For what it's worth,
There's more Bifidi in one inch of your colon
Than all the people that ever lived on Earth!"

"My oh my!
That's a whole lot of Bifidi!"

"It's our most important duty:
We make things happen in your booty.
We connect with the heart, with how you feel.
We connect with your brain, what a heck of a deal!"

We billions of Bifidi help with poop balance.
We regulate liquid, that's one of our talents!
We do all the things that good Bifidi do.
We help keep you healthy. We tend to the poo.

"Benny Bifidus, King of Poo,
You love the stinky things you do!
Your many tasks are so important:
You're a Gut-Heart-Brain Informant.

All your billions are in cahoots.
I'm glad I'm wearing these rubber boots!"

"Who is this rolling along, with all those odd little arms!?"

"That's Stanley Stem Cell, your repairman. He answers alarms."

"When things go wrong,
I'm just the right guy.
I go to the wound and multiply.

"We help make scabs! We're good boy scouts.
We're stem cell repairmen: that's what we're
about! We live in your bones. We travel through
your blood.
If you have an owie, with stem cells we flood!"

"Here we are – we all work together.
If you take care of us – we'll help you forever!"

"Hold tight! Hold tight!
We're going to take flight!
It's called 'Stem Cell-Gliding' – It's really exciting!
You'll enter your heart –
And your heartbeat will squeeze you –
To land in your lungs,
And your lungs, they will sneeze you!"

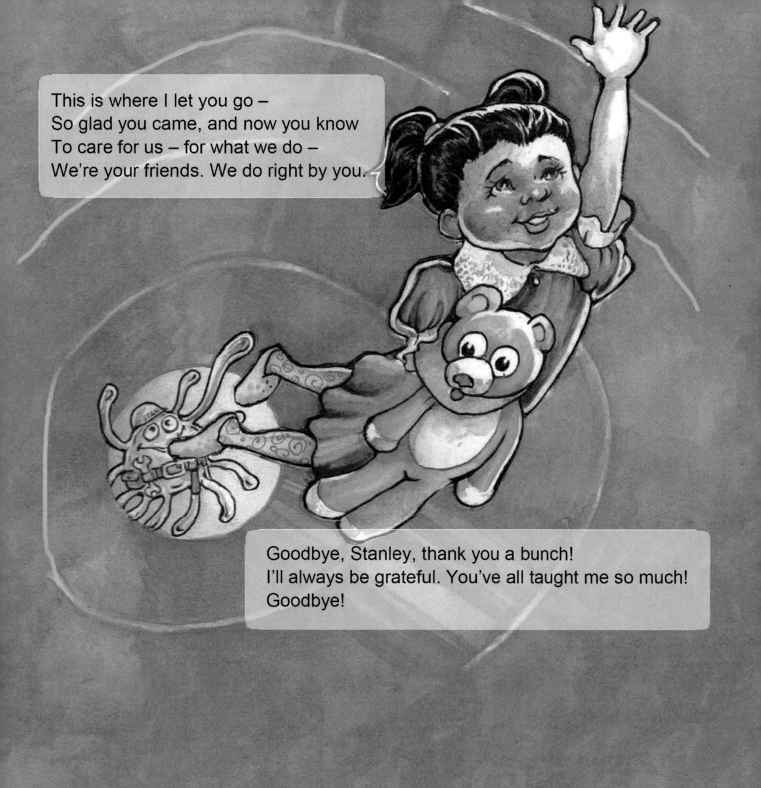

"ACHOO!"

GLOSSARY

ACIDOPHILUS – \ **a**-sa-**da**-fa-les – friendly bacteria living mainly in the small intestine – also the bacteria added to dairy products (as yogurt and milk)*

BIFIDUS – **bi**-fi-dus (singular) BIFIDI – **bi**-fi-dye (plural) – friendly bacteria living mainly in the colon (large intestine)

BIOTERRAIN – **bi**-o-ter-**rain** – the home where bacteria live

DIGESTION – dye-**jes**-chun – breaking food down into nutrients to be used for maintenance, growth and repair

DIGESTIVE ENZYMES – cells that produce certain chemical changes to speed the digestion process

GUT-HEART-BRAIN CONNECTION – The gut, heart and brain all communicate to work together – a recent scientific discovery. See the internet, including **www.chriskresser.com** and youtube.com

ILEOCECAL VALVE – il-ee-oh-**see**-kul – a door-like valve that separates the small intestine from the large intestine, or colon

INTESTINE/GUT – in-**tes**-tin – also known as the gastrointestinal tract – the 25-30 foot long tube from the stomach, which includes the small and large intestines. The intestine digests our food and eliminates waste.

IMMUNE SYSTEM – i-**mune** – the system that protects the body from disease and infections

NUTRIENTS -**new**-tree-ents – food

STEM CELL – a special cell formed inside of bones which is able to become all different kinds of cells in order to heal damaged cells

VILLI – **vill**-eye – little hills inside the gut wall that help move digesting food and waste farther down the gut

* The song "**Do the Acidophilus Hula**" is available from the author's website: **www.janmaxcon.com**

Made in the USA
Middletown, DE
05 December 2022